THIS WALKER BOOK BELONGS TO:

_____

_____

_____

_____

For Tricia, Van Morrison and my father
"...as big as a whale's love can be."

First published 1990 by Walker Books Ltd
87 Vauxhall Walk, London SE11 5HJ

This edition published 2003

10 9 8 7 6 5 4 3 2

© 1990, 2003 Simon James

The right of Simon James to be identified
as author/illustrator of this work has been
asserted by him in accordance with the
Copyright, Designs and Patents Act 1988

This book has been typeset in M Bembo

Printed in China

British Library Cataloguing in Publication Data:
a catalogue record for this book is available
from the British Library

ISBN 0-7445-9805-2

# My Friend Whale

## SIMON JAMES

WALKER BOOKS
AND SUBSIDIARIES
LONDON • BOSTON • SYDNEY

My friend Whale and I swim together every night.

My friend Whale is a blue whale.

My friend Whale makes the biggest splash,

but he is a very slow and graceful swimmer.

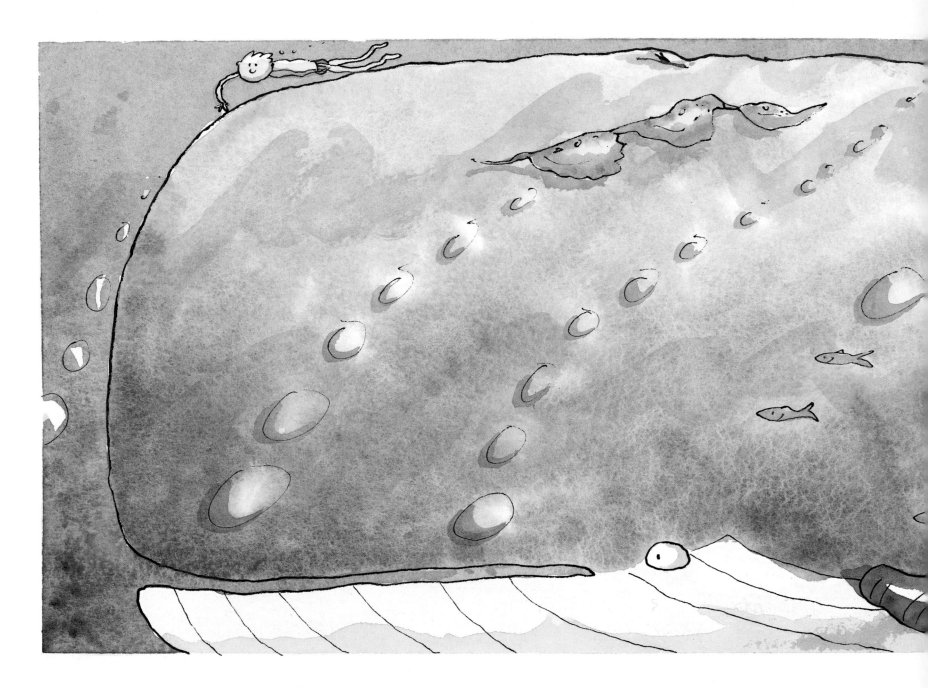

My friend Whale is the biggest and heaviest
animal in the whole world.

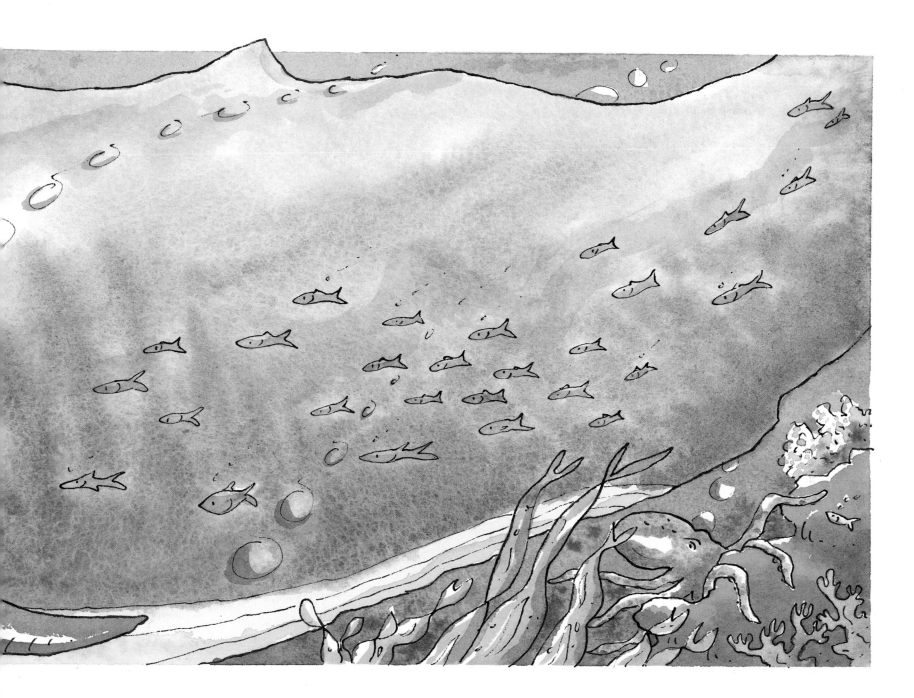

You may think, because he is so large, that he must be dangerous.

But my friend Whale has no teeth.

In fact he only eats fishy things smaller than my little finger.

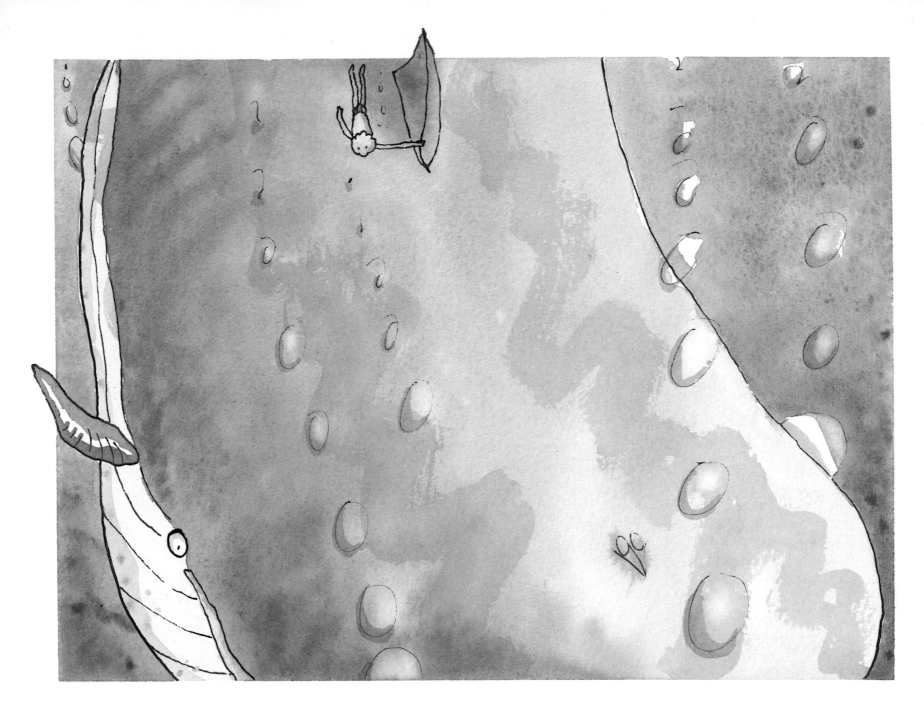

My friend Whale can hold his breath under the water for an hour,

but then he has to come up for air, just like me.

My friend Whale can't smell anything.
My friend Whale can't taste anything.

But he has very good ears – he can hear things that I can't.

My friend Whale talks with squeaking,
clicking and whistling sounds.

Other whales can hear him from a hundred miles away.

My friend Whale has very sensitive skin.
He can feel the slightest touch.

See you later, my friend Whale.

My friend Whale really does make the biggest splash,

but he hasn't come tonight.

He didn't come last night either, or the night before.

I'm afraid he will never come back.
What can have happened to my friend Whale?

My nights are empty without my friend Whale.

# BEFORE IT IS TOO LATE

Whales are peaceful.
Whales are gentle.
They do not hurt each other
and they do not hurt human beings.
But for hundreds of years
human beings have hurt whales.
So much so, that some kinds of whales
may soon die out altogether.

We have hunted whales for their meat.
We have hunted them for their bones.
We have hunted them for their oil.
We have killed more than two million whales
in the last fifty years.

In 1986 most of us agreed to stop. But not all of us.
Since then, another 22,000 whales have been killed.

We do not need whale meat.
We do not need whale bones.
We do not need whale oil.
We do need to care for whales.
We need them alive and safe
in the oceans of the world.

If you would like to help save the whales,

you can write to these places for information:

*Greenpeace UK* Canonbury Villas, London N1 2PN

*The Whale and Dolphin Conservation Society* Brookfield House, 38 St Paul Street, Chippenham, Wiltshire SN15 1LY

*The World Wide Fund for Nature* Panda House, Weyside Park, Godalming, Surrey GU7 1XR